DATE DUE   SEP 03

SEP 29 '03
JUN 29 '04

GAYLORD   PRINTED IN U.S.A.

D0602321

ARE WE THERE YET?

by **Dandi Daley Mackall**   illustrated by **Shannon McNeill**

Dutton Children's Books • New York

CIP Data is available.

Published in the United States 2003 by Dutton Children's Books,
a division of Penguin Putnam Books for Young Readers
345 Hudson Street, New York, New York 10014
www.penguinputnam.com

Designed by Tim Hall • Manufactured in China
ISBN: 0-525-47095-6
First Edition
1 3 5 7 9 10 8 6 4 2

I dedicate this book to Jen, Katy, and Dan . . . and all our
family car trips. So, are we there yet, guys?
—D.D.M.

To my family and friends, with much love and many thanks
—S.M.

Backseat race—
All in place?

Wagons ho!
Here we go!

City fading,
   Ducks parading,
Mooing cows all serenading.

Sing-along?
  Hate that song!
How long is "It won't be long"?

Got a feeling something's wrong . . . .

Are we there yet, Mom?

Boring,
  Snoring,
    Zilch to do.
Someone pinched me!
Wonder who?

Slumping,
    Bumping,
        Seat belt squeeze.
Let me out *now!*
    Pretty please!
Did you know our dog has fleas?

Are we there yet, Mom?

Slimy fingers,
   Smelly feet.
Help!
   I'm sticking to the seat!
Starving!
   Nothing good to eat!

Are we there yet, Dad?

Rest-stop exit?
  Fill 'er up!
Run in circles,
  Chase the pup!
Ice-cold pop—a giant cup!

Are we there yet, Mom?

Take a bite—
 Great food fight!
Scarfing everything in sight.
Tummy feeling
 Not quite right.

Are we there yet, Dad?

It's too hot!
  It's too cold!
Pretty sure I'm growing old!
Look! My sandwich
  turned to mold!

  Are we there yet, Mom?

Whooshing air,
 Trucker's stare,
There went brother's underwear.
Snickering,
 Bickering,
  Nothing's fair!

Stupid rain!
Where's our lane?
Is this Mexico or Maine?
Next time, can we take the train?

Are we there yet, Mom?

Wipers squeak,
  Windows leak,
Hypnotizing highway streak.
Sighing,
  Yawning,
    Cheek to cheek.

      Are we there yet . . .

...ZZZZZZZ ...

THE END

FREE
SPACE